Seldovia Sam

*To the young readers
at Community Library—
I hope you enjoy this.*

[signature] 2003

and the

Very Large Clam

WRITTEN BY
Susan Woodward Springer • ILLUSTRATED BY
Amy Meissner

Alaska Northwest Books®

To Liam and Amelia Springer-Aleksoff. Read, Dream, Live!
— S. W. S.

For Michael Dempsey, a cool Alaskan kid.
— A. C. M.

Text © 2003 by Susan Woodward Springer
Illustrations © 2003 by Amy Meissner

Library of Congress Cataloging-in-Publication Data

Springer, Susan Woodward.
    Seldovia Sam and the very large clam / written by
Susan Woodward Springer ; illustrated by Amy Meissner.
        p. cm. — (Seldovia Sam ; 1)
Summary: While clam digging with his father, Sam gets stranded on a small island while searching for the biggest clam he can find.
    ISBN 0-88240-570-5
    [1. Clams—Fiction. 2. Islands—Fiction.] I. Meissner, Amy, ill.
II. Title. III. Series.
    PZ7.S768465 Se 2003
    [Fic]—dc21   2002010730

Alaska Northwest Books®
An imprint of Graphic Arts Center Publishing Company
P.O. Box 10306, Portland, Oregon 97296-0306
503-226-2402
www.gacpc.com

President: Charles M. Hopkins
Associate Publisher: Douglas A. Pfeiffer
Editorial Staff: Timothy W. Frew, Tricia Brown, Jean Andrews,
    Kathy Howard, Jean Bond-Slaughter
Production Staff: Richard L. Owsiany, Susan Dupere

Editor: Michelle McCann
Book and cover design: Andrea L. Boven / Boven Design Studio, Inc.

Printed in the United States of America

Contents

1 The Too-Big Boots 7

2 Trip to the Clam Beach 12

3 Digging for Clams 19

4 Wrestling the Monster Clam 27

5 Stranded! 33

6 Sam's Rescue 38

7 Rescue of the Clam 45

8 Grime and Punishment 50

9 Time to Eat! 55

10 A Slimy Surprise 61

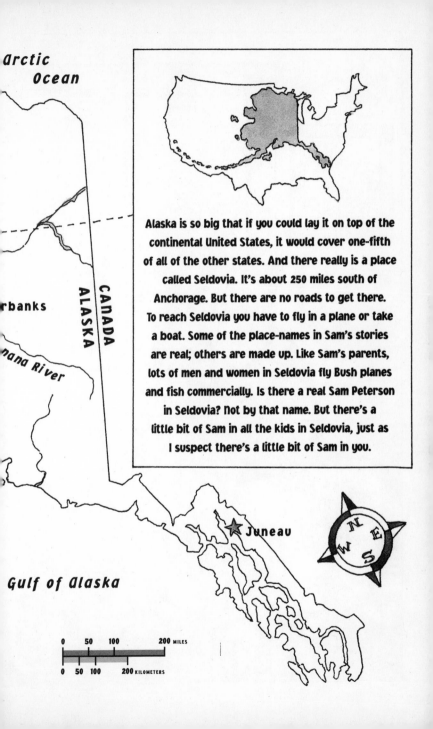

Arctic
Ocean

rbanks

nana River

CANADA
ALASKA

Alaska is so big that if you could lay it on top of the
continental United States, it would cover one-fifth
of all of the other states. And there really is a place
called Seldovia. It's about 250 miles south of
Anchorage. But there are no roads to get there.
To reach Seldovia you have to fly in a plane or take
a boat. Some of the place-names in Sam's stories
are real; others are made up. Like Sam's parents,
lots of men and women in Seldovia fly Bush planes
and fish commercially. Is there a real Sam Peterson
in Seldovia? Not by that name. But there's a
little bit of Sam in all the kids in Seldovia, just as
I suspect there's a little bit of Sam in you.

★ Juneau

Gulf of Alaska

N
E
W
S

| 0 | 50 | 100 | 200 MILES |

| 0 | 50 | 100 | 200 KILOMETERS |

1

The Too-Big Boots

Deep within his quilt and his scratchy-warm wool blankets, Sam turned over. He heard early morning sounds rising from the kitchen below. There was a soft low whistle, then the skittering of dog toenails on linoleum, and finally the door opening and closing.

It was Dad letting Sam's dog, Neptune, outside for her morning routine. Then Sam heard the *wh-h-r-r* of the coffee grinder and the clanking of pans on the big gas range.

Dad's footsteps fell on the stairs, and his

deep voice called, "Sam. Time to get up."

Sam burrowed farther under the covers and pulled the pillow over his head. It muffled the sound of his father's voice.

"Come on, Sam. The clams won't wait."

Sam was excited to go clamming with his father, but it was awfully hard to leave his warm bed.

Wh-o-o-os-s-h-h!!! Off flew the covers! Sam drew his legs up like a scared hermit crab as the cold air hit them. He opened his eyes, blinking.

Dad stood over him, smiling. "I know it's tough to get up, Sam, but we have to get moving or else we'll miss the good clam tide."

Dad handed Sam his clothes and Sam shivered as he hurried into them. He followed Dad down the narrow wooden steps and hopped across the cold floor on his bare feet. He scrambled up onto a stool next to Dad.

"Good morning, love," said Sam's mother. She placed a steaming bowl of oatmeal in front of him, and planted a kiss on top of his rumpled head.

"'Morning, Mom," replied Sam, as he dove into the oatmeal.

"I wish I could go clamming with you two, but I've got early flights today," said Mom. Sam's mother was a Bush pilot. She flew a small plane that carried people and supplies back and forth from Seldovia to the bigger towns across Kachemak Bay.

Outside the kitchen window, the sky was still dark. Sam could barely make out Neptune, waiting patiently on the porch. He washed down his oatmeal with a big glass of juice.

"I brought your new boots inside to warm up a bit," said Dad. "You'll want to throw on an extra pair of socks."

Sam stared at the shiny black rubber knee boots. *Ugh,* he thought. Sam grabbed two thick pairs of socks out of the dryer pulled them on his feet. He frowned as he slid his foot into one of the stiff boots. Even with two socks on, he could move his foot all around inside.

"Mom, these boots are so big," Sam complained. "I wish I could have a pair of hip-waders like Dad."

"Sam, we went over this yesterday," said Dad patiently. "Hip-waders are too expensive for a kid who's still growing. These knee boots are the smallest ones Mr. Murphy could find for you at the store."

"As fast as you're growing, those boots will be a perfect fit by next week!" teased Mom.

Sam smiled half-heartedly. He loved Seldovia, but sometimes not being able to drive to the big stores to buy exactly what

you wanted was a real pain.

How in the world would he be able to walk through the gooey clam mud in these clown-sized boots?

2

Trip to the Clam Beach

Time to load up, Sam. Grab your stuff and let's hit the road."

Dad pulled his wool coat from a peg on the wall, as Sam yanked a warm sweater over his head and shrugged into his canvas jacket. He lumbered out the door in the big rubber boots. Sam and Dad loaded the pickup truck: buckets, a sturdy shovel, a short-toothed rake, and a digging spade for Sam.

"Okay, Neptune," said Sam, "Up you go."

Neptune leapt into the truck and Dad

closed the tailgate. Mom juggled an armful of stuff and set aside her radio headset and big black flight logbook.

She handed them a thermos of coffee, one of cocoa, and a sack full of peanut butter cookies.

"Save these for later, when you're done digging clams. The wind is supposed to blow hard this afternoon so I suspect we'll quit flying early today. I should be home in time to help with lunch."

"Thanks," replied Dad as he kissed her and slid behind the wheel. "Be careful up there."

The truck pulled out onto the dirt road. As soon as they were out of sight of their house, Sam and Dad looked at each other, grinned, and without a word, opened the sack of cookies.

Carefully, Sam unscrewed the thermos lids and poured steaming cups of coffee

and cocoa. He knew to fill the cups only
halfway. One of his first jobs on Dad's
fishing boat was to fetch coffee from the
galley stove for Dad and the crew. If a
wave hit the boat a certain way, a full cup
of hot coffee could spill and cause the
men to say words that Dad thought a boy
Sam's age shouldn't hear.

The truck passed the Seldovia airstrip with its rows of Bush planes. Sam could hear an engine warming for the day's first flight across Kachemak Bay. Soon Mom would be there in her little blue-and-white Cessna, taking off from the dirt airstrip and soaring high over the sparkling water to Homer.

As Dad and Sam headed toward the clam beds at Jakolof Bay, the road dipped down into Dark Creek Canyon. The floor of the sunless canyon seemed like the bottom of the world. When the truck started up the other side of the canyon, the engine strained and sputtered. Dad had to set his coffee mug on the dashboard and downshift. The truck lurched and the empty buckets in the back fell over and rolled, crashing into the tailgate. Sam looked at Neptune. She stood nose into the wind, black ears flying. The noise didn't bother her. In fact, she looked as though she might even be smiling.

The road wound back up along the cliffs high above Kachemak Bay. On the left, the land dropped away and Sam could see the ocean far below. Dad slowed down so Sam could look at his favorite eagle's nest. Sam craned his neck to look for signs of life in the nest, but the eagles must have left already for a beach somewhere, feeding on an early spring run of salmon.

In the distance, a string of islands stood just offshore. Sam always recited their names for his father.

"Ready, Dad?" asked Sam.

"You bet, Sam. Go for it."

Sam took a deep breath and called out, "Herring-Hesketh-Yukon-Cohen-Sixty-Foot Rock!"

"Right you are, Sam," said Dad.

The road descended for several miles, and then, through the forest, Sam glimpsed the water of Jakolof Bay. The weathered boat dock came into view and Dad slowed down. A man working in a big wooden skiff straightened up and waved. It was Dad's fisherman friend, Gil Chambers. Up popped another head, a smaller one.

Oh, no, thought Sam. *It's Melody Chambers, the know-it-all queen of Seldovia Elementary School.* If Dad stopped to talk, Sam would be trapped! He'd have to be nice to Melody. YUCK!

3

Digging for Clams

Just as Sam had feared, his father brought the truck to a stop.

"Howdy, Wally. Taking the boy out clamming?" Gil called. Uh-oh, Melody was headed their way.

"Yep," answered Dad.

"I don't know why you even bother," chirped Melody, leaning against the truck window. "Those clams in Jakolof Bay are so puny. The ones on MacDonald Spit are much bigger. That's where I always go."

What a pain! thought Sam. Melody believed she was smarter than everybody, and she was always full of advice. Sam couldn't stand it.

"That's what you think . . ." he started, but his Dad elbowed him. Hard. "Uh, thanks for the tip, Melody. We'll have to try it there sometime," Sam finished.

Sam was disgusted as they pulled away from the dock. He resolved to find the biggest clam ever. That would teach Melody.

Dad pulled off the road and carefully eased the truck onto a dirt track. The truck tilted crazily as the tires climbed over some huge spruce roots. Then, suddenly, the track spilled them out of the woods and onto the beach. Sam loved the crunching sound as the tires rolled over empty clam and mussel shells.

The tide was very low. The exposed beach stretched almost halfway across Jakolof Bay. Rising from the beach were three little humps, each supporting a few spruce trees. At high tide the water would surround the humps until they became islands, but for now they were completely dry.

Dad let down the tailgate and Neptune sailed out. She wagged her tail, barked, and danced in excited circles. Dad handed a bucket and spade to Sam, shouldered the rake and shovel, and started walking.

Sam's new boots left huge prints in the sand. He put his bucket over his head, stretched his arms in front of him, and pretended he was a terrible, big-footed, bucket-headed monster.

Before long Dad and Neptune were far ahead. Sam tried to run to catch up, but in the big rubber boots his feet seemed to stumble over every single stone. Thankfully Dad stopped and Sam caught up.

"Well, this spot looks as likely as any," he decided. "Let's get to it!"

Dad began to dig. It looked like hard work to Sam. Soon Dad was pulling small white clams the size of little cookies from the mud at the edges of the hole. Sam helped, squatting

on his heels and picking out clams. In a nearby pool of water, Sam swished the mud from the clams and put them carefully in the bottom of the bucket, so as not to crack their shells. They seemed awfully little to Sam, but he knew they would be just right for chowder. He worked quietly alongside Dad until the big bucket was almost full.

I would like, thought Sam, *to find a very large clam.*

He looked up and down the beach. His gaze fell on the farthest dry island.

"I'm going to try digging by that island," Sam announced to his dad. *Surely I can find a very large clam way out there*, he thought to himself. *No one digs there, and I bet the clams grow huge*.

Dad laid down his shovel and looked at his watch.

"You'd best be quick about it, Sam," said Dad. "In fifteen minutes the tide will be turning to come in. Do you see that big rock there, the one with the driftwood log next to it?"

Sam nodded.

"Don't go past that rock, and make sure you keep an eye on the water. Okay?"

"Sure thing, Dad," replied Sam, as he tossed his digging spade in his bucket and scampered off down the beach. Neptune ran along beside him.

The receding tide had left pools of water, and Sam and Neptune splashed through just about all of them. A tiny ripple in one pool caught Sam's eye: it was a wriggling eel! The slippery eel was impossible to catch as it slid through Sam's fingers.

Just wait until I get my hands on a very large clam, thought Sam. *I won't let him get away.*

Sam turned over a rock in another pool and peeled off an orange starfish. Thousands of clear tube-legs waved gently in the air. He looked for a giant clam in the mud under the rock, but all he saw was a baby crab. He picked it up carefully and held it out to Neptune.

"Careful, girl—it's just a baby, but I'll bet it could still pinch your nose," Sam warned the sniffing dog. "Don't worry. Clams don't have pinchers."

Sam wandered from pool to pool, finding squishy nudibranchs, spiny sea urchins, and brittle sea stars. But no large clam.

Under every rock and strand of kelp was a new and glistening treasure. Sam passed the big rock and the driftwood log without even noticing them.

When would he find that clam?

Just as he was about to give up, Sam saw something near the last island. It was a huge stream of water shooting up from the mud like a geyser.

"Look, Neptune!" cried Sam, jumping up and down with excitement. "Could that be the squirt of a very large clam?"

4

Wrestling the Monster Clam

Sam grabbed his digging spade and raced to the spot. As he stepped on the soft mud next to the clam hole, another geyser shot up. *Whooosh!*

"Yeee-ha!!" hollered Sam. "This must be the king of all clams!"

Sam dug quickly. Neptune stood on her hind legs and snapped at the flying mud. The tip of Sam's spade struck something hard.

Could it be?

But it was only a rock. Sam pried the rock out and kept digging. He hit another

rock, and another, and another. Sam's arms were getting tired. As he dug, cold sea-water seeped into the hole, making it even harder.

Would he never find this monster clam?

Finally, Sam's spade scraped something . . . it felt like the edge of . . .

. . . another rock? More water gurgled into the hole and the soft muddy sides started to cave in. Sam scooped out the icy water as fast as he could. He wouldn't give up now. He was too close.

He found the hard object again. It was the edge of . . . *dig, dig, dig* . . . the shell of . . . *dig, dig, dig* . . . *oh, my goodness* . . . **A VERY LARGE CLAM!**

Sam threw down his spade and began digging out sand with his hands. He knew that the shell would break if he were care-less and hit it too hard with the spade. Breaking the shell of a clam would kill it, and Sam knew that dead clams are not safe to eat. Besides, how could he show off a broken shell to Melody Chambers?

He sat back on his heels to rest a moment. Sweat was pouring off him now. Even with the shell still partly buried, Sam could tell that this was the biggest clam he had ever seen. Neptune whined in his ear.

"Settle down, girl. We've almost got him."

Finally he was able to get his hands around the clam and pull. It didn't budge. The suction of the mud was too strong.

Neptune whined again and nudged Sam's arm with her nose. Sam pushed her away.

He gently worked the tip of his digging spade under the clam and pried up carefully. He scraped a little and pried a little. He scraped and pried a bit more, and then . . .

Sshhl-l-u-c-k! The clam popped loose

with a big smacking noise. Sam lost his
balance and fell down suddenly—*ker-
plop*—into the wet kelp. There, cradled in
his hands like a muddy jewel was . . .

A VERY LARGE CLAM!

It was bigger than his hand.

It was bigger than both his hands
cupped together.

It was even bigger than the foot of
Sam's boot!

Sam stood up triumphantly and said,

"Come on, girl. We'd better get going. The tide will be coming in soon ..."

But Neptune was gone.

As Sam turned toward shore, he saw his bucket float by. The big rock and the driftwood log were gone, covered by fast-rising water. The water was now between him and the shore.

Oh no! thought Sam, *I'm trapped!*

5

Stranded!

Sam took a few steps toward shore. His boot sank in the soft muck and wouldn't budge. Bone-freezing water poured over the top and ran down inside, soaking his sock! Sam yanked his leg as hard as he could. Out popped his bare foot, his sock left behind in the stuck boot.

Just as Sam was about to panic, he heard Neptune. She was standing on the third hump, which was now an island completely surrounded by water, and she was barking at him frantically!

"There you are, girl!" Sam said with

relief as he wallowed toward the island. Barnacles and broken shells stabbed at his bare foot, but he was too scared to stop. Finally, he fell exhausted onto the beach next to his dog.

He caught his breath and glanced around. To his great dismay, he realized they were stranded!

Sam looked across the rushing water to the shore. He saw the tiny figure of his father, bent over his clam hole. Sam cupped his hands around his mouth and yelled,

"H-e-l-p . . . Da-a-d . . . He-e-l-p!"

Nothing.

He might as well have whispered. The wind and the roar of the incoming tide drowned out his voice. Sam tried again, yelling until the last squeak of air had left his lungs.

"H-E-L-P . . . DA-A-D . . . HE-E-L-P!"

Far away, his father stood up and looked in Sam's direction. Sam jumped up and down, waving his arms wildly. His poor foot landed on more sharp things, but Sam barely noticed. Dad gestured and waved back. Sam stopped jumping and listened hard.

"Sta-a-y put, Sam. I'll go get he-e-l-p!"

Sam picked up his digging spade and his clam and climbed higher onto the little island. The water was still rising all around him. He sat down in the long yellow grass. His bare foot was icy cold and was bleeding where the broken shells and the barnacles had sliced the skin.

Neptune flopped at his side and put her head on his knee. Sam watched the tiny figure of his dad hurriedly gather up the clamming gear and run for his pickup. The truck, so small it looked like a toy, raced up the beach and disappeared into the woods.

Sam stood and turned in a slow circle. It seemed like just minutes ago that the whole bay was one big beach. Now there was water everywhere! The current swirled as the tide rushed in, carrying a mess of brown seaweed and smooth driftwood.

Sam wondered how high the water would rise.

Would it cover the top of the little island before Dad could bring help?

6

Sam's Rescue

Sam felt his insides squeeze in panic. Then he remembered how to read the high-tide line. Dad taught him once when they were fishing in the bay.

Sam stretched out on his stomach and leaned over the edge of the island. He peered down at the ledge below, and there, halfway up, was a scummy green line. Below that line, the rocks were dark with algae from the sea water. Above the line, the rocks were pale gray.

Sam was pretty sure he would be safe here even at the highest tide. At least he hoped so. He sat back down in the grass, hugging his knees to his chest, and shivered. He had gotten pretty wet digging up that clam and his bare foot was aching from the cold. He shivered again, and pulled Neptune close. Overhead an eagle hung in the sky. As it flew beneath the weak spring sun, its shadow washed over Sam. It made him feel even colder, and very alone.

Sam's stomach growled . . . loudly. Neptune pricked her ears and cocked her head at him. *What I wouldn't give for one of those peanut butter cookies,* thought Sam.

Then a new worry began to gnaw at him.

He had disobeyed his father!

He went beyond the big rock and didn't pay attention to the tide. Worse, he lost a brand new boot, not to mention a bucket!

I'll bet Dad is furious, thought Sam. *I'll*

probably be grounded ...forever!

Then new worries crept into Sam's head. Maybe Dad drove too fast and the truck ran off the road! Maybe he couldn't find a boat at the dock! Sam was getting hungrier and colder by the minute.

Neptune bolted up and stared intently

past Sam. Straining, Sam could hear the faint drone of an engine. He jumped up, but his sore foot made him sit right back down.

"Hooray! Here comes Dad!" cried Sam.

He watched and listened, but the noise flew overhead. It belonged to a little plane.

Maybe it was Mom, and she didn't even know he was stranded down here. Tears welled in Sam's eyes, and he rubbed them away with his fist.

"I will never, ever disobey Dad again," vowed Sam, " . . . if only . . . if only . . ."

Then, the whine of another engine caught his ear. Slowly, it grew louder and louder as Sam stared harder and harder out at Jakolof Bay. Then, there it was! In the distance, a skiff was heading toward the little island. As it got closer, he could make out two figures.

One of them was Dad!

The engine changed to a lower pitch and the boat slowed. Dad's face was a mixture of anger, worry, and relief, but he threw Sam a grin.

"Someone here call for a taxi?" called out Gil Chambers, who was driving the boat.

Sam was so happy he wanted to cry.

Gil brought the boat around to the sloping side of the island as Neptune barked and wriggled in greeting. Dad hooked one leg over the side of the boat, hopped out, and waded onto the beach. His strong arms swooped down and gathered up Sam. Neptune leaped into the boat, skidding across the wooden seat. Gil shifted into reverse and backed the boat away from the island.

Dad rumpled Sam's hair and kissed the top of his head. Sometimes Sam felt like kisses were for little kids, but not today. He nestled against Dad's chest. He was glad they hadn't brought Melody.

"Sam, what happened to your boot?" asked Dad.

Oh yeah, thought Sam, his happiness ebbing away. *The boot.*

"It got stuck in the mud and the water came in and I couldn't move and I pulled as hard as I could and my foot flew out and the boot stayed stuck," explained Sam, all in one breath.

Dad was puzzled. "What in the world were you doing way out there? I told you not to go past the big rock."

Sam hung his head and stared at the floor of the skiff.

"I saw this big clam squirt and so I ran to dig it up. You wouldn't believe it, Dad. It's huge . . ."

Suddenly Sam realized that he had forgotten the clam and his spade back on the island!

Oh, no! thought Sam. *All that digging and freezing to death for nothing!*

7

Rescue of the Clam

The awful look on Sam's face told Dad everything. The two men exchanged glances. Gil winked at Sam, turned the skiff around in a tight arc, and headed back toward the little island.

"Thanks, Gil. We owe you one," Dad said with a sigh. He seemed about as tired as Sam.

Gil cut the engine and tilted up the outboard motor to clear submerged rocks as they drifted up to the island's beach again. Dad jumped out and pulled the bow of the boat onto the sand.

"Stay here, Sam. I'll find them," he said.

From the skiff, Sam directed his father to the yellow grass at the top of the island. Dad quickly found the digging spade and the prized clam. He returned to the boat and pushed off. Gil started the engine with a single sharp pull of the cord.

Dad held up the muddy clam and stared

at it, as if it were the clam's fault all this had happened. Then he lowered the clam over the side of the boat and into the water.

Was Dad going to drop the clam back into the bay? Was that going to be Sam's punishment?

When Dad's hand came back up with the big white clam still in it, Sam realized he was just rinsing it off. Phew! Sam tried not to crack a smile. He knew he was still in big trouble.

Dad pulled a wool mitten from his coat pocket and carefully slipped it over Sam's foot. It felt scratchy, but warm.

Gil nosed the skiff up to the Jakolof dock and Dad climbed out to tie the bow-line. Gil cut the engine and tied up the stern. Melody stood on the dock with her arms folded, looking down at Sam. He couldn't meet her eyes. He just KNEW she'd make some smarty-pants remark.

"Thanks again, Gil," said Dad, "I'm glad you were here."

Gil grinned, "I was ready for a break anyhow, Wally. Happy to help."

Gil paused from lighting his pipe. "Sam, do you think I could take one more look at that giant clam of yours?"

"Sure," said Sam. He looked at Dad,

who reached into the pocket of his coat. Out came the clam. Even in Dad's big hand, it still looked huge.

"Wow!" exclaimed Melody. "That's the biggest clam I've ever seen!"

Sam smiled to himself. She must have forgotten her claim that ALL the clams in Jakolof Bay were puny!

Dad reached his big hand into the skiff and pulled Sam onto the dock. Then he crouched down.

"Climb up on my back, Sam," he advised. "You shouldn't walk on that foot."

"So long, Gil," Sam called as they headed up the dock. "And thanks … for everything."

Gil lifted a hand in salute. Dad opened the door of the truck and deposited Sam on the seat. The truck was warm from sitting in the sun, and suddenly Sam felt very sleepy.

8

Grime and Punishment

Sam slept all the way back to Seldovia. He slept as they passed the islands and MacDonald Spit. He slept as they passed the eagle's nest and Dark Creek Canyon. He even slept as they passed the airstrip, now busy with planes taking off and landing.

Then something shook him awake.

"Come on, Sam. Climb aboard. We're home."

Sleepily, he wrapped his arms around his father's neck as he was carried into the house.

At the sight of his mother frowning in the kitchen, Sam finally woke up.

She'd ground him for sure!

But Mom didn't say much. She dragged a dining room chair in for him to sit on and fussed over his foot. Dad brought in an old washtub that Mom filled with warm water and Epsom salts.

"Put that foot in here, Sam, and don't you move it an inch. Do you understand?"

Sam nodded solemnly. He stared at the water as the grime and sand melted

off his foot.

"I'm going outside to help your father unload the truck."

Great, thought Sam. *They're going to figure out some horrible punishment for me.*

Sam stared into the washtub. His foot stung and throbbed all at the same time. He hadn't realized how sharp those clamshells and barnacles could be.

The kitchen door opened and Mom and Dad came in with the bucket of clams.

Uh-oh, here it comes, thought Sam.

"Your father and I have decided ..."

Now, I'm really in for it.

" . . . that your sore foot should slow you down long enough to think about your disobedience," said Mom. "And you had a good enough scare being stranded on that island, so we're not going to ground you."

That's it? wondered Sam. *I can't believe it!*

"However," Dad continued.

Uh-oh, the dreaded "however."

"If you're going to work with me on the boat someday, you're going to have to learn to respect the tide and the sea. The tide doesn't slow down just because you're having too much fun playing in the mud. You're also going to have to learn to listen and follow instructions. I can't have a deckhand who doesn't pay attention."

Sam nodded miserably. He dreamed of deckhanding for Dad when he was older. He was mad at himself for acting like a little kid. Still, this was pretty light punishment.

Maybe if he looked really sorry and pathetic, he could get off with just the lecture.

Not so lucky.

9

Time to Eat!

Mom looked stern as she said, "Sam, for the next six weeks, you'll be forfeiting your allowance to help pay for a new pair of boots."

"Yes, Mom," mumbled Sam.

There went his spending money for an upcoming class trip to Homer. Oh well, he thought, it could be worse.

"I've got to rinse down the tools and check on the boat," Dad said to Mom. "If you'll make lunch for us hungry clam-hunters, I'll fix a chowder for dinner."

"Sounds good," replied Mom, "as long

as you throw in your buttermilk biscuits."

"It's a deal," smiled Dad.

Sam watched Mom work. She steamed the giant clam in a little water until the shell opened and the clam inside was firm. Then she cleaned dark green algae out of its stomach and chopped the clam into pieces.

"Sam, this really is the biggest clam I've ever seen," said Mom. "Imagine — one clam feeding three people for lunch!"

She dipped each piece in beaten egg and then rolled it in bread crumbs and cornmeal. In a heavy cast-iron skillet, Mom heated bacon grease until it sputtered. Then she tossed in the pieces of breaded clam and fried them until they were golden brown.

Dad stamped his feet on the mat and came through the kitchen door: "Smells great in here!"

He sat down and Mom gave them each a small heap of fried clam. Sam's very large clam was absolutely delicious — hot, buttery, and salty fresh like the sea.

After lunch, Dad rubbed stinky ointment into the sole of Sam's foot and wrapped it in a clean, soft piece of old sheet. Sam helped him shuck all the little clams for the chowder they would have for dinner.

Dad set a big pot on the back of the range and brought a little water to a fierce boil. He placed handfuls of clams in the pot until their shells steamed open wide. Then, he removed them with a big slotted spoon into a bowl to cool.

Using a small knife, Sam scooped the clams out of their shells and into another bowl.

Next, Sam helped his mother chop potatoes, onions, carrots, and celery. Dad

strained some of the cooking water from the clams into a bowl, then rinsed out the big pot and set it back on the range. Dad cut up a slab of bacon and browned it in the pot with some garlic and the onion and celery. Then, he added the potatoes

and carrots and the cooking water from the clams.

When the potatoes were soft, he dumped in Sam's bowl of shucked clams. Dad grabbed a can of creamed corn from the pantry and added it to the pot. Mom chopped fresh parsley, and shook in rosemary and dill. Then on went the lid, and down went the heat.

Last but not least, Dad stirred in rich canned milk. Together with his homemade biscuits, this was the tastiest dinner Sam could imagine!

Things were definitely looking up, thought Sam. *Not only did I get off with light punishment, but as a bonus, I managed to lose one of those awful boots!*

10

A Slimy Surprise

That evening, as Sam and his parents sat down to eat, there was a knock at the front door. Dad pushed his chair back and opened the door. Gil and Melody stood there grinning.

In Melody's hand was a bucket, and in Gil's, a sodden black boot!

The rubber boot that looked so shiny and new this morning didn't look so shiny anymore. It was all drippy and slimy. Sam couldn't imagine putting his foot into something so gross!

"Melody and I were up the bay just

now checking on my net, and guess what she found washed up on the rocks?" Gil chuckled. "A boot and a bucket! I figured I knew who they belonged to!" he continued, winking at Sam. "Didn't find your sock though."

"Uh, thanks a lot, Gil." Sam thought that if his missing sock looked anything like the boot, it would be just fine with him if it was NEVER found!

Melody looked triumphant. This was definitely worse than being grounded!

Gil happily accepted Mom's invitation to join them for dinner. Melody slid into a chair beside Sam.

"Well, Sam, good luck for you," said Dad.

What could he mean? thought Sam. *It certainly wasn't good luck that Miss-Melody-know-it-all was staying for dinner!*

Dad and Mom looked at each other and nodded.

Uh-oh, now what? worried Sam. He'd had just about enough punishment for one night.

"Now that six weeks' allowance money can go toward buying you a pair of hip-waders," Mom said with a grin.

"I already have hip-waders," said Melody to no one in particular.

But Sam wasn't even listening to her. Hip-waders! He could hardly believe his ears!

"That is, as soon as you outgrow your lucky boots!"

They all laughed, even Melody, and Sam thought, *What a great day: a giant clam AND new hip-waders.*

Life for a boy in Seldovia didn't get much better than this!